Macy Goes to School

Written and Illustrated By:
Christine Kuschewski

This book is dedicated to my students. Thank you for making Macy's day at school so fun!

Today is an exciting day. Macy is going to school with her mom. Macy has her backpack and is ready to go!

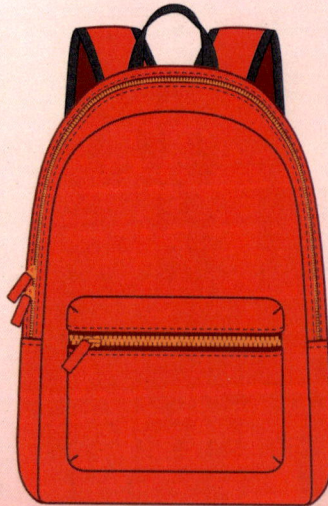

Macy and mom arrive at school. They go to her mom's classroom. Macy looks around. Then she sits and waits for the kids to come.

Macy's first class is math. She is working on fractions. Macy puts parts together to make a whole. She is doing great and working hard.

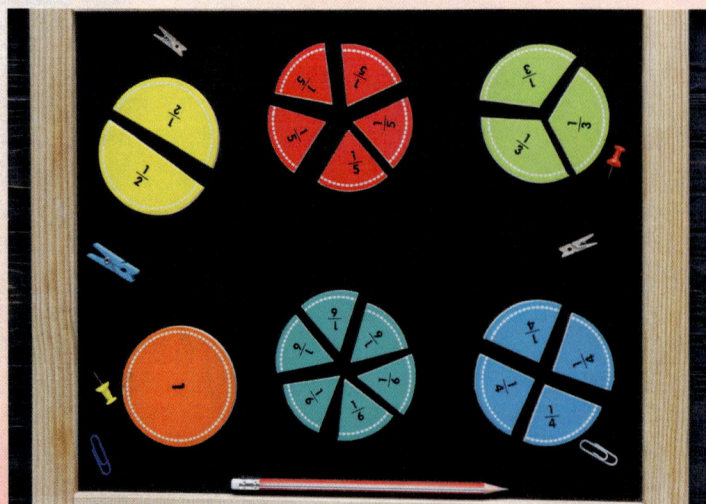

Next, Macy has writing class. She works on her writing. Macy is writing a story about her mom. Macy works hard during writing class.

Macy takes a break and goes to see the school. She visits the nurse's office. The nurse helps kids who are hurt or sick. She checks their temperature. She gives them ice if they have a bump. Macy likes to visit the nurse.

Next, Macy visits the office. The phone is ringing and there are many people in the office working. Macy quickly says hello before leaving for the library.

Macy and her mom go to the library. "Look at all the books!" says Macy. Macy wants to look at all the books, but her mom says they need to get back to class. "We can come to the library on another day," says her mom.

Macy's next class is reading. She sits at the table with her mom. The group reads the book together, and they answer questions. Macy likes the story. She listens as the kids read.

Soon it is lunch time. Macy and her mom go for a walk. They see the Kona Ice truck. "Can I have some, mom?" asks Macy. Her mom says dogs cannot eat Kona Ice.

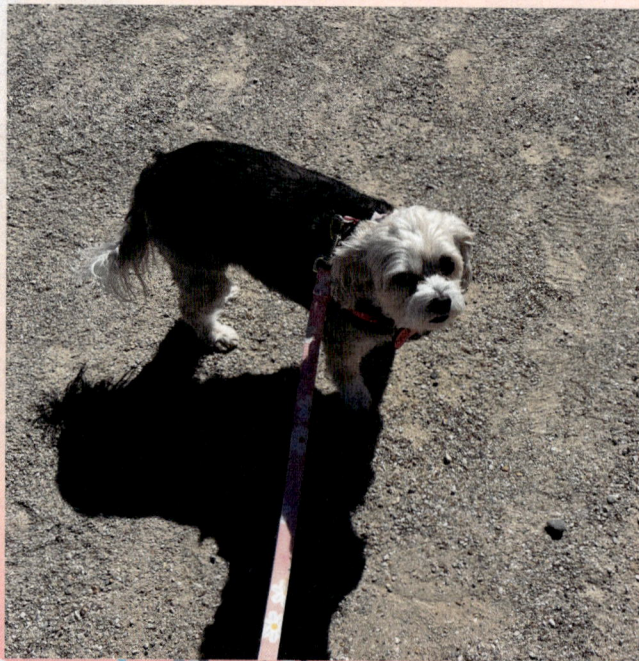

Macy and her mom go to the playground. Macy goes under the tire. Next, Macy goes on the slide. She climbs up. She slides down. Macy jumps off.

Macy and her mom go to visit the Little Red School House. Macy sits on the steps for a picture. "Mom, this building is very old," says Macy.

"Yes, this is the original school. It was built in 1926. It is 96 years old," replies her mom.

After lunch, Macy goes to the computer lab for tech class. She sits at the computer and listens to the teacher. She does her work. Macy is a good student.

Macy and her mom go back to her mom's classroom. The kids come in to read with Macy. They read to her. She reads to them, too. Macy loves to read!

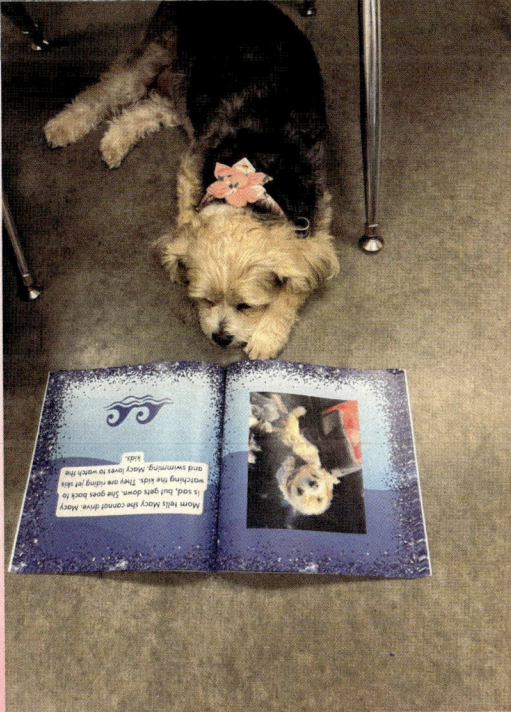

Macy is tired. She tells her mom that school is a lot of work. "It is almost time to go home," her mom says. "I'm ready to go home and take a nap," replies Macy.

zzz

The bell rings, and it is time to go. Macy had fun at school. She cannot wait to go back again, but she is tired and ready for a nap. Macy says good-bye to everyone and heads to the car with her mom.

Macy's World Titles

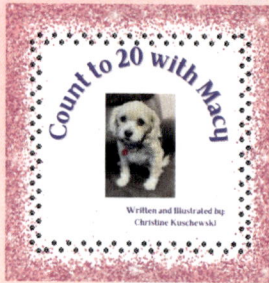
Count to 20 with Macy
Written and Illustrated by: Christine Kuschewski

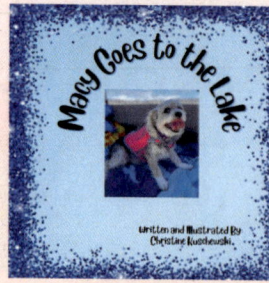
Macy Goes to the Lake
Written and Illustrated By: Christine Kuschewski

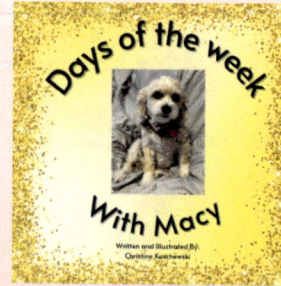
Days of the week With Macy
Written and Illustrated By: Christine Kuschewski

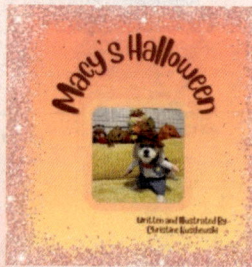
Macy's Halloween
Written and Illustrated By: Christine Kuschewski

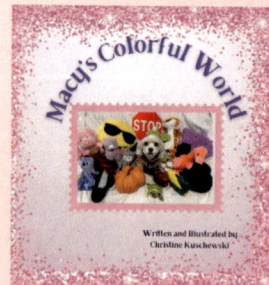
Macy's Colorful World
Written and Illustrated by: Christine Kuschewski

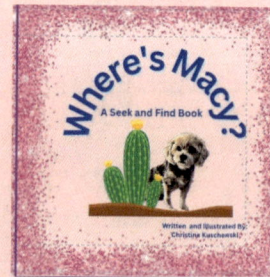
Where's Macy?
A Seek and Find Book
Written and Illustrated By: Christine Kuschewski

Months of the Year With Macy
Written and Illustrate By: Christine Kuschewski

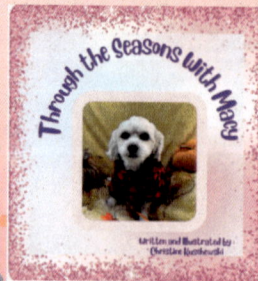
Through the Seasons With Macy
Written and Illustrated by: Christine Kuschewski

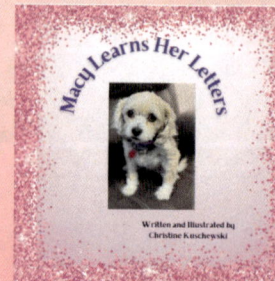
Macy Learns Her Letters
Written and Illustrated by Christine Kuschewski

Christine Kuschewski has been a special education teacher for 22 years. She loves teaching children how to read. Her love for books and education has led her to writing children's books.

Christine and Macy live in Arizona. Macy loves to spend time with her best friends, Toby, Kona and their family. Macy is a 7 year-old Bichon Frise, Poodle, Maltese and Shih-Tzu mix. Everyone who meets Macy falls in love with her. Together Christine and Macy enjoy spreading love to the world.

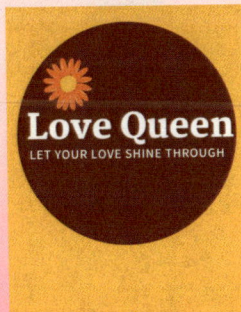

Love Queen

LET YOUR LOVE SHINE THROUGH

Made in the USA
Columbia, SC
23 November 2022